GOODNIGHT CANTON

PRO FOOTBALL
HALL OF FAME

by Mike Vivalo
Pictures by Jonathan Bartlett

AuthorHouse™
1663 Liberty Drive
Bloomington, IN 47403
www.authorhouse.com
Phone: 833-262-8899

Because of the dynamic nature of the Internet, any web addresses or links contained in this book may have changed since publication and may no longer be valid. The views expressed in this work are solely those of the author and do not necessarily reflect the views of the publisher, and the publisher hereby disclaims any responsibility for them.

Any people depicted in stock imagery provided by Getty Images are models, and such images are being used for illustrative purposes only.
Certain stock imagery © Getty Images.

This book is printed on acid-free paper.

ISBN: 978-1-6655-3427-7 (sc)
ISBN: 978-1-6655-3426-0 (e)

Library of Congress Control Number: 2021916187

Print information available on the last page.

Published by AuthorHouse 09/07/2021

authorHOUSE®

GOODNIGHT CANTON

PRO FOOTBALL
HALL
OF
FAME

by Mike Vivalo
Pictures by Jonathan Bartlett

AuthorHouse™
1663 Liberty Drive
Bloomington, IN 47403
www.authorhouse.com
Phone: 833-262-8899

Because of the dynamic nature of the Internet, any web addresses or links contained in this book may have changed since publication and may no longer be valid. The views expressed in this work are solely those of the author and do not necessarily reflect the views of the publisher, and the publisher hereby disclaims any responsibility for them.

Any people depicted in stock imagery provided by Getty Images are models, and such images are being used for illustrative purposes only.
Certain stock imagery © Getty Images.

This book is printed on acid-free paper.

ISBN: 978-1-6655-3427-7 (sc)
ISBN: 978-1-6655-3426-0 (e)

Library of Congress Control Number: 2021916187

Print information available on the last page.

Published by AuthorHouse 09/07/2021

authorHOUSE®

GOODNIGHT CANTON

By Mike Vivalo
Pictures by Jonathan Bartlett

In Canton Ohio
There is a building
With legends in its halls
And a picture of...

Pete Rozelle holding two footballs

There's Jim Brown who
scored 106 Touchdowns

And there's Moss and Elway and the legend
of the Steelers Immaculate Play

There's a group of 27 QB's

That will soon add Brady
and Brees

And autographed Dukes

And Barry Sanders jukes

And Ditka and Fouts
and Jerry Rice's routes

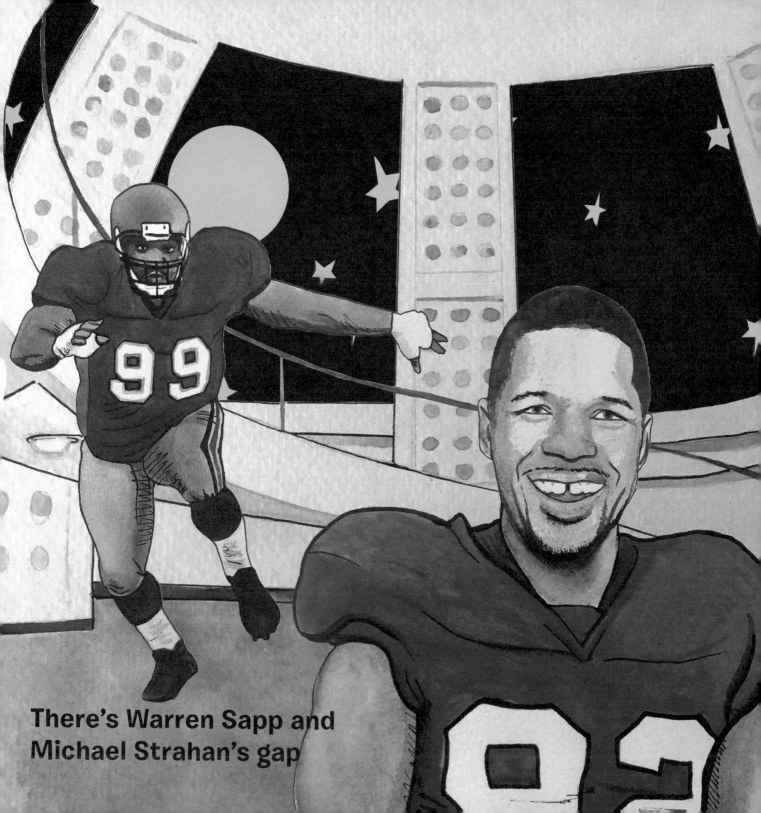

There's Warren Sapp and
Michael Strahan's gap

And hundreds of bronze busts, all collecting dust

Goodnight Canton

Goodnight Halls

Goodnight Pete Rozelle holding footballs

Goodnight Jim Brown
Goodnight Touchdowns

Goodnight Unitas
Goodnight Tony G

Goodnight Namath's
Super Bowl Guarantee

Goodnight Don Shula and
Lynn Swann

Reggie, Deion and Marino's arm

Goodnight Urlacher's blitz

Goodnight L.T.'s hits

Goodnight Coach Lombardi
Goodnight Marcus Allen

And Goodnight Video Game
Legend John Madden

Goodnight
Ladainian Tomlinson

Who scored 28
TD's in just one
season

Goodnight Walter Payton

Goodnight Terrell Owens

Goodnight 1972 Miami Dolphins

Goodnight Dickerson's Glasses
Goodnight Polamalu's Hair

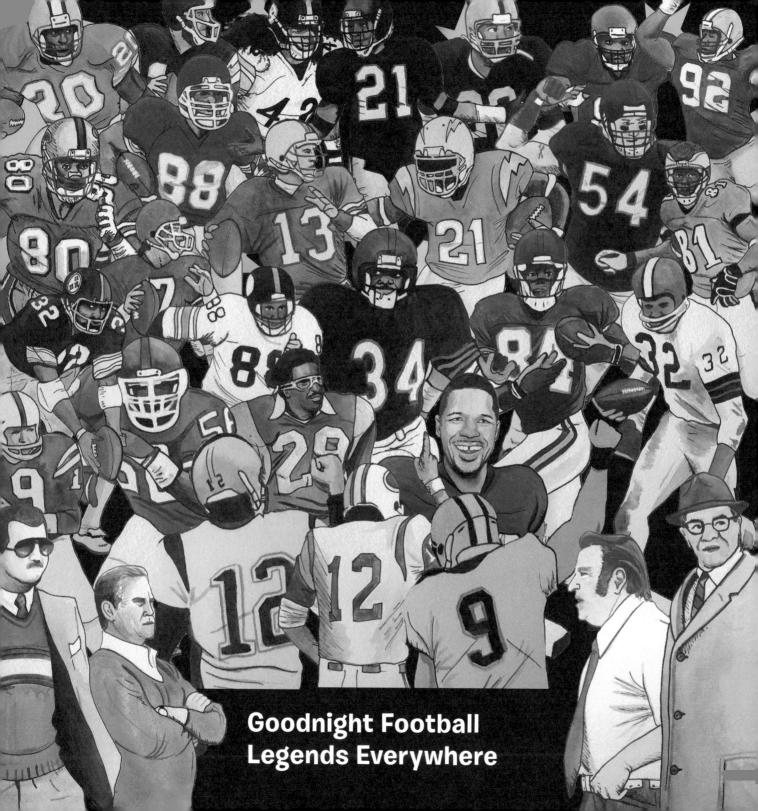

**Goodnight Football
Legends Everywhere**

Printed in the United States
by Baker & Taylor Publisher Services